Heathcote Williams

JOHN CALDER
LONDON
RIVERRUN PRESS · DALLAS

Other plays by the same author

The Speakers

The Local Stigmatic

Malatesta

AC/DC

Remember the Truth Dentist

The Supernatural Family

PlayPen

Hancock's Last Half Hour

First published in Great Britain 1978 by
John Calder (Publishers) Ltd.,
18 Brewer Street, London W1R 4AS
First published in the U.S.A. 1978 by
Riverrun Press Inc.
4951 Top Line Drive · Dallas 75247 · Texas

All communications regarding the performance of this text should be addressed to the author's agent: Emmanuel Wax, Actac Ltd., 16, Cadogan Lane, London, S.W.1.

ISBN 0 7145 3714 4

Cover and book designed by Richard Adams
Typeset in Aldine Roman by Open Head Press, Notting Hill
Printed in Great Britain by Hillman Printers (Frome)Ltd.

THE IMMORTALIST

The Immortalist was first performed at the Oval House, Kennington with Neil Cunningham as The Immortalist and the author playing The Interviewer. The play was later presented at the Crucible Studio, Sheffield with Ken Shorter as The Immortalist, Andrew Norton as The Interviewer and directed by David Leland.

The play was inspired by a conversation between David Solomon, Mike Lesser and the author, with additional contributions from David Leland, John Mackay and Robert Anton Wilson.

The Set: A television studio. Arc lights, video monitors, two studio cameras.

VOICE OVER: No one needs telling that time is the handservant of death, but the sniff of insurrection is in the air. Death itself perhaps is doomed to fall victim to time.
We have secured the following interview with one of a small but highly organised advance guard. He is two hundred and seventy eight years old.

INTERVIEWER: Why do you insult the average life-span with your longevity?

278: I've discovered the secret of time.

INTERVIEWER: What is the secret of time?

278: That there is no time. Time is a false alarm.

INTERVIEWER: How did you smash your biological clock?

278: I stopped it from running.

INTERVIEWER: It's said that they smashed all the clocks

during the Paris Commune. Do you remember that?

278: Sure. It was my idea, and Courbet was in on it too.

INTERVIEWER: Wasn't that perhaps a mistake? Weren't they in Frazer's terminology...Frazer, the Golden Bough..

278 *(nods).*

INTERVIEWER: Weren't they mistaking an ideal connection for a real one?

278: I'd rather have an ideal connection than a real one any time.

INTERVIEWER: So you would say that the ideal should be timelessness?

278: The ideal **is** timelessness. Life's too long for time, time's too short for life.

INTERVIEWER: How do you attain this state of timelessness?

278: Tell yourself this every day: Every day, in every way I become less and less timeful. If you do it every day it has a diurnal and cosmic effect - and it makes you feel 24 hours younger.

When I was born two hundred and seventy eight years ago, I was something of a prodigy. I knew where I'd come from: I could see up the nozzle of my father's cock for seven generations - and I knew where I was going to. The pearly gates? what are they? a memory of the vaginal orifice. I knew how to regress and evolve at the same time...

INTERVIEWER: That sounds like meta-gibberish.

278: *(laughing)* You make me feel 120 when you say things like that.

INTERVIEWER: But if there's no time, then there's no beginning and no end. Don't you find that horrifying?

278: As you look out of your eyes now you have only about 160 degrees of vision, that's why you see beginnings and ends. I have 360 degrees.

INTERVIEWER: So you're saying that time is just my lack of perception? But why do things stop and start?

278: They don't.

INTERVIEWER: You mean everything is moving?

278: Yes. I can hear it. Can't you?

INTERVIEWER: O.K. *(pause)* Who do you think invented death?

278: It's an exploitation device invented by some earth-bound spiv to keep you coming and to keep you going. It fucks up your bio-rhythms. It's the final rubber stamp. It certifies that you've been totally exploited. They also plant a carved rock on the top of your chest to indicate that there's no point in anyone else trying to exploit you. Death comes like a thief in the night– **Don't let yourself get mugged!**

INTERVIEWER: What is the secret of immortality?

278: It's a secret, but it's only a secret from those who don't know.

You see: we're microcosmic. We have everything inside us and we always will. We have God and we have God's son. God's son descends from us. Falls down from what comes into us. Does that give you a clue?

INTERVIEWER: No.

278: Think of Jesus who was spat on and reviled. What distillation of us is spat on and reviled?

INTERVIEWER: Crap?

278: Exactly. Within your own excrement is the secret of immortality.

INTERVIEWER: Could you be more specific?

278: The substance is called **indole.**

INTERVIEWER: Uhuh. Aleister Crowley ate his own excrement and he's well dead.

278: Crude attempts. He didn't sublimate it. He just let it hang.

INTERVIEWER: Will you tell us how to prepare it?

278: Sure.

INTERVIEWER: But aren't there any conditions? Do you want everyone to have this formula for immortality?

278: Sure.

INTERVIEWER: Even Richard Nixon, for example?

278: Would he want it? Death is for the deadly.

INTERVIEWER: O.K. Immortality in a turd. Lay it on the line.

278: Soak a turd in petroleum ether and add water; the soluble excrement will separate and you can obtain the sublimated shit which contains **indole**, packaged chemically in **Di-Methyl-Tryptamine** and **Di-Ethyl-Tryptamine**—two powerful psychedelics. Immortality is a trip!

INTERVIEWER: Oh, come on...

278: It's just one method. How to live forever with no expensive props.

INTERVIEWER: All right, but what's the point of infinity

if there's nothing that's finite?

278: I can see that it might give infinity a bit of local colour. But **Istigkeit ist die einzige arbeit.** Isness is my business. Meister Eckhardt.

INTERVIEWER: He told you that?

278: In his way. He was German at the time.

INTERVIEWER: But if there's simply a continuous present, what is the reason for the concept of time?

278: It's a bureaucratic and scurrilous attempt to chart pain. There's no time for time – I told you. Big Ben is Big Brother's Brother. Ticks are tics that bite your brain.

Everything happens an infinite number of times as well as not happening at all. Imagine a giant fly-wheel: every -thing spinning, everything repeating. Now as well as this perfect repetition, there's the vibration of the machine. That's what you mortalists perceive and that's what you are. What you mortalists think is real is no more than a slight and irrelevant imperfection in the cycle of infinite recurrence. Valve trouble caused by your presence.

INTERVIEWER: You mean that reality and time are produced by a fault in some timelessness machine? that sounds like nonsense.

278: Time is nonsense, your consensus reality is nonsense,

and they both lead to death. Time, as you mortalists would have it, is merely an accumulation of your faulty perceptions of timelessness. Everything you measure is altered by the act of measuring it. Heisenberg probably rules – O.K.? Serial time, linear time, cumulative time–none of them get behind it and they all dim your mind's eye. Don't let Father Time kick sand in your face.

INTERVIEWER: You mean we're blinded by time?

278: Of course, and death is your whole body gone blind. It's your perverted awareness of time that incites death, which is merely a bad habit–a suffocating accumulation of bad habits. It's an incident which happens so often that people have learnt to accept it, but there is no accidental death: accidents are incidents with an axe to grind. There's **no** accidental death whatever the circumstances. Death is always suicide. Lose your sense of time and gain a sense of timing.

INTERVIEWER: You mean that death is no more than a fashion?

278: It's a weak dogma kept up for the sake of appearances. I saw Albert Camus shortly before he allowed himself to be killed in a car accident, and he said: "The relationship between the murderer and his victim is the only true relationship." How decadent can you get?

INTERVIEWER: But surely the victim doesn't **choose** to be murdered?

278: With the exception of myself and a few others of my ilk still circulating, every human being ever born on this planet has been murdered, consented to be murdered and spent their entire lives preparing for that pointless little spurt so beloved by footling existentialists.

It's time for Life and Death to get divorced, maybug. At the moment you're just an unwanted bastard from the Life-Death marriage. Join up now, baby– there may not be a later.

INTERVIEWER: Do you ever imagine yourself dying?

278: Do you ever imagine being shat on by a pterodactyl? No. I don't... Not unless I goof, like Old Tom Parr.

INTERVIEWER: The old man who's buried in Westminster Abbey?

278: Yes, he's locked up there. He lived to what? from 1483 to 1635. He lived on ale and sour cream.

INTERVIEWER: How did he die?

278: He was invited to a celebration feast given by the King... to celebrate his 152nd birthday. They fed him larks' tongues, pigs' trotters in aspic... all the 17th Century delicacies. Twelve courses—all of them meat. Poor Tom was too polite to refuse. A life-long vegetarian. All that meat completely butchered his system and he popped his clogs the next day.

INTERVIEWER: I take it from that that you're vegetarian?

278: I eat meat if it meets me. Just carrion. I take what nature gives me. I don't rip it off. Maybe that's why Adam and Eve blew it – it suddenly occurs to me – they took the fruit off the tree before the tree was ready to give it to them.
Perhaps we should decapitate all florists. Butcher butchers?

The Animal Kingdom and the Plant Kingdom, you see, they're the Fourth World. Now you've been expending a lot of energy on the Third World because you can vaguely understand its starving death rattle, but the Fourth World has no pushy philosophers, no politicians. Nevertheless, they can fly higher, run faster, make more useful produce, communicate more quietly and more successfully and waste fewer resources than their colonial masters. "The meek will inherit the earth." What do you think that means?

The Fourth World's given up striking back with lions and tigers: they're all in jail, all in zoos or circuses. They've got a strike force now which consists of an almost infinite number of almost invisible guerrillas. More people die from insect produced diseases than from any other cause.

You should make peace soon, otherwise you're going to have to accept some very punitive terms.

INTERVIEWER: But we don't die simply because we're ripping off the Fourth World, as you call it?

278: It's a contributory factor. Here's another Fourth World lesson. You know how lizards lose a leg, lose a tail, and it grows again?

INTERVIEWER: Yes.

278: Well, why haven't we got that facility?

INTERVIEWER: You mean even **you** don't?

278: I'm working on it. I have a few clues. But the reason most of us don't have it is that we're somatically involutionary. The reason we don't have it is that it would put all the warmongers and doctors out of business. The reason we don't have it is because we **asked** not to have it.

DNA—which is evolution's little CIA agent—whispered to the powers that be, that people really **want** to hurt each other, they really **want** to paralyse each other, they really **want** to maim each other, so they cloned it out of us, this facility, and left us as amputees. They did what the human race asked them.

INTERVIEWER: So if we ask long enough for immortality we'll get it?

278: Naturally. DNA, which is part of you, is immortal, so you can be. It's time you wised up. DNA is just using you as an idiotic robot to create more DNA. And it's the same with all species: as soon as they can fuck and consequently produce more DNA, they start to die. Look at the salmon—it dies immediately after spawning.

INTERVIEWER: Could one paraphrase it then by saying that DNA is a spiral out to screw us?

278: Uhuh–but it works in billions and billions of years; so a lot of people have got to start screaming at it before it changes its tune.

INTERVIEWER: What do you mean "screaming at it"?

278: I mean **screaming.** I mean saying **"I'M NOT GOING TO DIE!"**
"Ask not for whom the bell tolls, it tolls for thee." Familiar? Less familiar: "Man has created death," W.B.Yeats, and each person's death doesn't just diminish you, it's a direct **attack** on you.

Death is an infectious and insidious larval reaction to negativity, which turns you and your life into a soap-bubble. You think death is a random, stochastic process that you can't control? **Crap.** It's a curable disease. The hand of God is at the end of your wrist. All you've got to do is change the programme– change the station your body is listening to.

The universe is an intelligence test. How much do you think you're going to score by dying?

When I visited Einstein (shortly before he had his relatives snort his ashes: he has no known grave, and that is what happened), he showed me some of his journals in which he'd written: "the fear of death is the most unjustified of all fears, for there's no risk of accident to someone who's dead–or not yet born." Interesting, huh?

This is what I mean: If you tell your body "I'm going to die," "I'm afraid of dying," your DNA's just going to get the very best out of you before you do. It's going to cream the scene before you blow it. But if you say to yourself: I just had a tip-off, death is a rip-off and we're all going to live forever, till our bodies turn to leather–then your DNA's going to be forced, sooner or later to sign a treaty with you and your body, and let you into some of its secrets...

INTERVIEWER: What sort of secrets?

278: Well, it's been around for a long time. What do you think the Kundalini is? a double helix. What is the Caduceus? Mercury's wand–with two snakes spiralling round? a double helix.
DNA has had its portrait painted by Babylonians, Hindus and Greeks, and it's even represented in the lay-out of Irish burial grounds.
The mathematical sign for infinity? *(drawing ∞ in the air)* **The nucleotide template**–the double helix.
The Witches' Dance–especially when they perform the Dark Rite of Osiris, which confers immortality–is almost always an inward-turning, double-stranded spiral.

INTERVIEWER: But what secrets have **you** learned from it?

278: I'll tell you one. The earth is a living, breathing organism which you mortalists are slowly snuffing. Amputating its lungs, injecting unspeakable filth into its bloodstream, invading its digestive system, and perverting its precious glandular secretions so that they poison they air...

all self-evident, right?

INTERVIEWER: Yes.

278: You relish hearing that other people have died because that seems to put off the moment of your death—you kill each other out of some pathetic cargo-cult fantasy that it will lengthen **your** life, but it doesn't, and then you think that maybe if you kill the **whole planet** and offer **that** up as a gigantic sacrificial scape-goat (and with your low-minded mortalist politics, of course you won't be around to suffer the consequences...)

(shrugging his shoulders) I don't know. I'm not a specialist in irrationality...

Anyway—the secret—DNA got its head together with an ambassador from the Plant Kingdom, and I mean HEAD. H.E.A.D. Hedonic Engineering and Development... and both of them conspired to get some chemicals into you that would teach you some ecological sense. Haven't you noticed that people eating Amanita Muscaria, magic mushrooms, psilocins, psilocybins, peyote cacti, and smoking hemp on a massive scale has **exactly** coincided with the advent of ecological concern?

There's a tale your biology master never told you.

INTERVIEWER: Well, yes.. I suppose that's true *(looking towards the technicians)* I just hope it doesn't get bleeped out.

Do you think then that death has no social function?

278: Some people will do anything to get attention.

INTERVIEWER: But don't you think that your physical immortality casts aspersions on spiritual immortality?

278: They're the same thing. At the sub-atomic level matter is spirit, but even if you still think that they're not the same thing, having both has to give you a wider choice.

INTERVIEWER: For a man of 278 you are in remarkably fine physical condition–how have you achieved this?

278: Analyse. Transcend.

INTERVIEWER: Have you ever been ill?

278: Disease is simply being ill at ease. I connect.

INTERVIEWER: Over the centuries there has been a lot of documentary evidence to support the theory of re-incarnation, and recently it has even gained a certain respectability in academic circles through the work of Dr. Ian Stevenson...

278: Professor of Psychology at the University of Virginia.

INTERVIEWER: That's right. He's documented over 1,60 cases from all over the world... Birthmarks corresponding with injuries received in a previous lifetime and so on.
If re-incarnation rules, O.K., then why resist the proce

278: Re-incarnation is fairly chaotic. It's a kind of cosmic pyramid-selling. Good fucks lure down good spirits. Bad fucks lure down bad spirits—for re-incarnation purposes. And most fucks are pretty paltry: someone comes back from a hateful job thinking **Fuck** the Boss, **Fuck** everything—Fuck **You**. What kind of a concep -tion is that going to lead to?
A lot of low spirits lurking round the basements and cellars of the first astral plane are constantly being attracted by the exchange of stale and vitriolic hormones for their re-incarnation. Very few high spirits are being lured down by the exchange of abracadabra orgones.
How we fuck is who we are, and most people fuck like mindless jack-hammers on the blink. They haven't the faintest idea of what they're doing—but the results of what they do are transforming the whole nature of the planet.

Physical immortality enables you to stay permanently with the whole trip, instead of having your life confiscated every five minutes and having to scuff around the no-osphere and the far-gône-osphere looking for two people who are really getting it on, in order that you can get back into the action.

INTERVIEWER: Life can't exist without death; it's well known.

278: Oh come on, do you think I'm doing you out of life by abolishing death?

INTERVIEWER: Bernard Shaw said that there would have been no evolution without death?

278: When did he say that? on his death bed?

INTERVIEWER: I don't know.

278: Well, I imagine what he meant by it was that nature needs a dead-line to work to—in order to change for the better. But don't you think more fruitful changes would come if you had a **life-line** instead?

When I saw Shaw in America he was stuffing Hamburgers down his throat as fast as they could hand them to him. Couldn't resist the novelty. Died on his return. Tom Parr Junior.

I think what you've quoted is pretty insipid. He doesn't feature in my commonplace book.

INTERVIEWER: Who does?

278 *(reeling them off): "There is no death,"* Longfellow. *"Death! thou shalt die,"* John Donne. *"We know this much, Death is an evil, we have the Gods' word for it: they too would die if Death were a good thing,"* Sappho. *"And what do you expect a dead man to do with his body in the grave?"* Antonin Artaud. *"Death is dead,"* Shelley. *"Death only dies,"* Swinburne. *"There is not* **room** *for death,"* Emily Bronte. *"So shalt thou feed on death, that feeds on men, and death, once dead, there's no more dying then,"* Shakespeare. *"The last enemy that shall be destroyed is death,"* St.Paul. *"There are persons who*

have been exalted to God, and have remained in that state of exaltation and they have not died," Paracelsus. *"King Death hath Asses' Ears,"* Thomas Lovell Beddoes. *"Man will never be contented until he conquers death,"* Dr. Bernard Strehler. *"Mobilize the scientists, spend the money, and hunt out death like an outlaw,"* Alan Harrington. *"We should live longer than we do. Death does not seem essential to an organism. We are secreting poisons, but if they are taken away and our bodies kept clean, there is no reason why we should die,"* Sir Oliver Lodge. *"The fear of death has been the greatest ally of tyranny past and present,"* Sydney Hook. *"Some people want to achieve immortality through their works or their descendants. I prefer to achieve immortality by not dying,"* Woody Allen.

INTERVIEWER: *"I hate quotations. Tell me what* you *know,"* Ralph Waldo Emerson.

278: Immortality– from Calvary to Chemistry.

INTERVIEWER: What has been most peoples' reaction to you?

278: What would you think it was?

INTERVIEWER: Well, I should think it ranges pretty wide. From people thinking you're a complete and utter crank to their thinking you're some kind of U.F.O.

278: Never trust anyone under a hundred.
I pass fairly unnoticed. This planet is my manor.
I've never been physically outside it.
Frank–Frank Drake–who's professor of Astronomy

at Cornell, thinks incidentally that the secret of longevity can be learned from space aliens who are trying to communicate with us, and he just wrote in the Technology Review published by M.I.T., that he now believes that the majority of advanced races in this galaxy **have** immortality.

INTERVIEWER: I've heard of him. He's no bumbling Mister Natural.

278: And nor am I, if that's what you're implying. I'm not selling some Polyanna philosophy.

INTERVIEWER: You never get bored?

278: No one drills holes in me. I'm always being fed. I'm a hungry boll-weevil and the world is my granary. Sometimes my diet's dull–sometimes there's a lot of starch. I just look for another restaurant. But there's so much to **learn**–how can you possibly just jack it in and feed your brains to an unappreciative mortician?

INTERVIEWER: Do you seriously believe that there's no time? this interview's been going on for some time...

278: It's just been going on. There's no time for time, I told you.. I'm not being flippant. You want to look at it scientifically? O.K., prepare for a minor lesion in the left cerebral hemisphere.
The scientific definition of a second is 9,192,631,700 cycles of the frequency associated with the transition of the two energy levels of the isotope Caesium 133.

Get it?
On the other hand one Indian culture I ran into in Upper Pradesh uses the time to boil rice as the smallest basic unit.
It's all a tiresome mania.

INTERVIEWER: How did it start?

278: Clocks started in German monasteries which were really the first factories. The first official was the time-keeper and from him you had that necrophiliac lie that Time is Money. Clocks and capitalism are totally symbiotic. From the walls of the factory to the walls of the coffin. Wasting time was simply cheating the time-keeper.

Waste time and save yourself. Set your clocks back for ever. Freedom runs counter-clockwise.

INTERVIEWER: How did clocks start here?

278: The first working clock in this country was at Hampton Court. It was nick-named the Death Clock.
Some people are allergic to watches, did you know that? I'm not talking about people who wisely stop them running and can't wear them because of their own strong magnetic field, but about people who actually suffer radiation burns when they wear a watch.
And the computer? what's that? simply an uppity clock.
You remember the Death Knell? that was the only time the church clock could be interrupted. It meant that clocks had no further interest in you. Tick, tick, tick... it's death's descant, and digital watches

are death's dominoes.
Every time you wind your watch you screw yourself.
The faster you go the slower your watch goes. Einstein's special theory has been proved with atomic watches in manned satellites. The Fitzgerald-Lawrence ~~connection.~~ contraction.
The astronaut's watches hardly moved.
So keep bopping. Don't let anyone tie you down and you'll live longer.

When I was in China with Professor Joseph Needham...

INTERVIEWER: Immortality seems to be a name-dropper's paradise.

278: Look at it in the light of any of your preoccupations.

When I was in China with Professor Needham we went to a generator factory in Nankien, and they'd torn down the clocking-in board—there was just a rectangular shadow on the wall. People came to work when they felt like it, and worked only when they were peaking. A lot more got done.

INTERVIEWER: What are the other advantages of immortality?

278: It makes Green Shield stamps finally worth something.

INTERVIEWER: That's a little whimsical.

278: Look, biochemistry has made death an offer it can't refuse, and you want to refuse it, why?
You heard about the Last Supper? now find out

what's for afters. Or join the human race and die for a living.
THEY WANT YOU DEAD!

INTERVIEWER: Who do you mean by **they**—the proverbial **they?**

278: The Necropolitans. The forces of Awe and Boredom.

They know where you are when you're dead. You can't fool them any more. You can't keep changing your address. It's the ultimate steady job. All they need is a map reference.

INTERVIEWER: Can you tell us what you think of cryogenics—freezing people? do you think it'll work?

278: **Freeze—Wait—Re-Animate!** Sure it'll work. It's worked before. Spores in the ice. It's working in nature now: Crypto-Biosis—secret life. There's a species of small brine shrimp: **Artemia Salina,** to give you its name in Latin slang, that can encyst itself when conditions are negative, and then comes back to life again when conditions are favourable... in ten minutes or in ten years.

There's another called the **Tardigrade,** which normally exists in damp mud, but if its surroundings become de-hydrated it simply turns off all its life-support systems and to all intents and purposes it's dead. It can be heated to over 150 degrees Centigrade (far above the boiling point of water), and frozen to minus 200 degrees—but when it chooses to bounce back to life it does so—after anything up to a hundred and twenty years. It can switch on and off almost indefinitely.

Ears of corn that were found next to a mummy in the pyramids were planted and sprouted 3000 years later.

INTERVIEWER: But did anyone ever try planting a mummy?

278: We still have Pharoahs don't we? Gettys, Rockefellers, Rothschilds...
No—the Egyptians just embalmed their bodies without much ingenuity. Their prospective resuscitation was an expensive fantasy—whereas the Chinese were more sophisticated. In the **T'ao Hung Ching**, alchemical gold—that is gold transmuted by cinnabar was placed in the thirteen orifices of the body, and when that was done properly the body came back to life after exhumation.

Chinese Pharoahs were successfully planted.

INTERVIEWER: What is cinnabar?

278: Red mercuric sulphide, which can be made inside the human body, mainly by the distillation of sperm.

INTERVIEWER: And what about women?

278: I believe that fellatio has a certain popularity.
Nicholas and Pernelle Flamel lived on the tantric exchange of each other's bodily fluids, transmitted by nameless wildness, for 120 years each.

The alchemical furnace that you should use to produce the elixir is your own body. The Taoist immortalist

Page 27, the following line should appear between lines 4 and 5: "and intestines, and it is there that the embryo of"

hangs himself upside down like a bat, causing the essence of his sperm to flow to his brain. The famous fields of cinnabar in alchemical literature, the **tan-t'ien,** are to be found in the most secret recesses of the brain immortality is alchemically prepared. **Jesus gave you the product–now we give you the formula!**

INTERVIEWER: So there are more recipes for immortality than eating your own shit?

278: Sure. Try an apricot kernel to start with. The Pectin turns transmuted sperm into apricot jam. Delicious. That'll see you through to 130–and keep an eye out for the **Immortalist Cookbook** which a colleague of mine is working on.

Here's another: in Indian alchemy mercury is regarded as the sperm of Shiva and called **Narabya.** In the **Survana Tantra** you can find out how, by eating fixed or 'killed' mercury, called **Nasta Pista,** you may become immortal.

INTERVIEWER: How do you 'fix' mercury?

278: Let me quote you from the **Rasanarva**: *"When quick-silver is killed with an equal weight of purified sulphur, it becomes one hundred times more efficacious; when it is killed with twice its weight of sulphur, it cures leprosy; when it is killed with thrice its weight of sulphur it cures mental languour; when it is killed with four times its weight of sulphur it removes grey hair and wrinkles; when it is killed by five times its weight of sulphur, it becomes a panacea for all the ills that flesh is heir to..."*

Dead men of the world unite—you've nothing to lose but your lids!

INTERVIEWER: It still seems cranky to me.

278: Knees are knocking in mortuaries all over the world. The market value of death is going down all the time. Latest figure - six feet. Why do you pretend to have been still-born by dying? Death is a grave mistake.

Listen, if a hundred years ago when people were dying at thirty, you'd said that in a hundred years time the life-expectancy would be seventy, everyone would have said you were gaga—right?

INTERVIEWER: Right.

278: Look at it now though: the way life-extension is progressing even on a banal medical level. Within thirty years there's going to be an exponiential leap in life-expectancy to hundreds of years. For instance, if you're in your twenties now, you expect to die around 2026. Add the thirty years bonus to that and you expect to die around 2056. And how many years will science be able to give you by then?
Even assuming that the researchers currently speaking of life-extensions of hundreds of years are doing so too soon, in 2056 an increase of a hundred years will be a conservative projection. So you can live on to 2,156—and where will the life-extension sciences be **then?**

INTERVIEWER: You presumably count yourself amongst these researchers you mention?

278: I do, but do you want to know who they all are?

INTERVIEWER: Yes.

278: Well, there's Dr. Johan Bjorksten who in 1973 spoke of extending the human life-span to 140 years. Now he's confidently talking about 800 years. Then there's Paul Segall of the University of California, at Berkeley, who's experimentally stopped the ageing process in laboratory animals, and he believes that his work will extend the human life-span to between four and five hundred years before 1990.
Dr. Robert Phedra puts the number even higher. He says that we can begin aiming to extend the human life-span to 1000 years. How does that grab you?

INTERVIEWER: Well, I suppose they can't all be bananas.

278: No. Death sucks.

The Russians are injecting de-hydrated placentas into people desirous of longevity—and they believe that it'll extend their life-span almost indefinitely... but anything that can be done chemically can be done by other means.

INTERVIEWER: What do you mean?

278: I mean that you're constantly stimulating a different chemical mandala in your body— whatever you do. Even if you do nothing. There's a chemistry of nothing. There's also a chemistry of self-knowledge. Self-knowledge stimulates a large range of neuro-peptides...

INTERVIEWER: I can understand pain, or anxiety, or very strong emotions such as anger, stimulating chemical activity - pain, I believe stimulates endomorphines in the body, morphine derivatives...

278: Right.

INTERVIEWER: But compared with pain, self-knowledge is pretty abstract?

278: Are you sure you've tried it? your brain cells are dying off, hundreds every minute— whereas they have the same chemical ability to repair themselves as the other cells in your body which do do so.

If you obey alien orders, particularly for money, your brain cells die like scurf. You're not using your brain. You're rail-roading it.
Know-Thyself-Neuropeptides... to put it slightly glibly, will redeem the self-repair triggers in the neurones and the glia which have atrophied.
Take your choice. Cats know themselves. Animals very rarely goof. In an animal which has starved, or been starved to death, its brain is the last organ to go. Its brain will be in perfect condition, but you mortalists' brains are dying all the time...
Even in an Olympic athlete, at the peak of physical condition, his brain is half-dead. Why? because he doesn't really know what he's doing, or why.

It's time you gave death the cold shoulder—or squeezed the life out of it.
Look at Shakespeare—he was a touch before my time...

INTERVIEWER: Just a touch.

278: About the width of a cigarette paper. But look at the sonnets. Written when he was about thirty, and obsessed with decay, senility and death. Why? because it was **happening** to him... aged thirty. And he went downhill from then on. Ridiculous.

INTERVIEWER: Do you believe that Jesus Christ conquered death?

278: Yes and no. He survived clinical death for a very brief period. But having done so he didn't have much juice left over to do anything. Why not? well, in his life-time he'd blown several fuses by cursing fig-trees, sending pigs to their death, and giving people craven advice such as Render Unto Caesar That Which Is Caesar's. Just look at what he did after the Resurrection: wobbled around like a wraith for a couple of weeks and then floated away. He was completely unrecognisable to his friends, and he'd hardly got the strength to say good-bye to them. He died.

INTERVIEWER: Are you ever tempted to think that you're God?

278: I'm just in the kindergarten of the Immortalist Movement. The Universe is the Messiah.

INTERVIEWER: There's a graffiti I've seen written up from time to time: *"Death is nature's way of telling you to slow down."* How does that strike you?

278: If it makes you laugh, it's true.

INTERVIEWER: It didn't make you laugh.

278: It's rather sad. If you don't do what you want to do—you die. What could be simpler? that's the thought behind it.
Death is just DNA getting fed up with you. Your nervous system is a robot operated by a genetic pilot called DNA, but you mortalists are afraid to look at the pilot... just like you behave on aeroplanes: you never look at the pilot. If you did, it might undermine your confidence.

INTERVIEWER: So death is a kind of DNA hi-jack—a DNA putsch?

278: Yes. It's your body's immunity system jacking it in. Why? because your anti-bodies have finally picked up the message from a mainly hostile world: *Give Up—What's the Point?—Pack it in—Don't Move—* **Surrender!**

INTERVIEWER: I get the feeling you're a little bit patronising about cryogenics—freezing people? am I right?

278: It's perfectly possible, but why spend your life in a fridge lumbering people with your electricity bill?

INTERVIEWER: When you say it's possible, do you really think it's going to work?

278: Oh yes. The thing is going to work. Ettinger froze

sperm in 1964 and revived it...

INTERVIEWER: Get 'em by the balls, and their hearts and minds will follow?

278 (*smiling)*: Yeah. From now on it's just a question of scale.
Head transplants... which I understand they prefer to call Body transplants... the whole schtick.

But it's just shutting the stable door after the horse has bolted, and who is going to be frozen? Who's going to be revived? the kind of money that has to be conned for research is going to ensure that you have a nation run by immortal Rockefellers, Rothschilds and Gettys.

And then people are smashed up in car accidents, let's say, and have to be frozen in bits and pieces... well, who gets transplanted to whom... mmmn? What bit to what bit? Dr. Frankenstein would come in his grave.

I find it all very funny. Poor old Walt Disney in the Snow Queen's palace in Disneyland: there's one room that the tourists aren't allowed into, with hoar frost leaking from under the door. That's where he is—a giant ice-cream; and apparently before he shacked up in this frozen fairy-land, he made a whole series of films for Disney employees. They're shown to the staff each month. Just Disney rapping—telling them not to draw genitals on any of his characters, and to keep celebrating the Great American Virtues—and then he ends up waving at them and saying, with an icy glint in his eye, "*I'll be* **seeing** *you.*"

INTERVIEWER: Won't a world filled with people who live as long as you have, multiply the world's problems by some enormous proportion?

278: Am I a problem to you?
(throwing up his hands) Problems. Problems are just D.O.R.

INTERVIEWER: D.O.R.?

278: Deadly Orgone Radiation.
People with problems are merely acting as witting or unwitting receptors for D.O.R.

INTERVIEWER: Why?

278: Because they're dying and therefore attracting negative energy. Look at cancer—another fine growth industry. There's a huge collaboration between all these so-called sufferers. Let me tell you, a problem shared is a problem doubled... They're all pooling their bad news into a huge throbbing, palpitating sump in an attempt to give the whole planet Electro-Shock Therapy, because they think there's something wrong with it...

INTERVIEWER: There's an old Arab saying: *If you rescue a man from drowning, you have to look after him for the rest of your life."* Would that summarise your attitude, which I must say I find pretty indifferent?

278: If you like, but what's an Arab doing drowning in the desert? Look, I'm from Aristocrats' Lib...

INTERVIEWER: I've gathered that.

278: Stay hungry, stay foolish. You want me to spend every day in dog-shit because of your demented ideas of what constitutes a social conscience? Listen, people foul up because they stay in the same place. They've traded utopia for reality. They've traded their instinct for politics. Consuming is a substitute for being... There's a woman: Deva Mehta in Rajasthan, who hasn't eaten or drunk for fifty years—she lives off sunlight: condensation and salts in the air... You have radio as a substitute for telepathy, television as a substitute for astral projection. Aeroplanes are a substitute for levitation. Smoking is a substitute for inner fire. Reproduction is a substitute for immortality...

INTERVIEWER: I might pick you up on that one.

278: Can you reach that high? One of the purposes of lovemaking (not that you can make love—love **is**) is to achieve immortality... When it fails, you get conception.

And what else is wrong with you mortalists? you consume instead of feel. You have God instead of Aeon Juice.

INTERVIEWER: What's that?

278: **Go with the Glow and Renew the Glue** and you'll find out. Mobility is the most revolutionary tactic there is, and what is more revolutionary than the conquest of death? **what is more revolutionary?** Marxist-Leninist misery? "please, dear Government, we'd like, with your permission, to negotiate a higher rate of exploitation for this wonderful opportunity you're giving us to shorten our lives?" (I knew that impenetrable little punter Karl when he lived in Dean Street—spent all his spare change on Stock-brokers... a little known fact). Bakunin? he spent most of his time ingratiating himself with White Russians... and Proudhon? "Property is theft."? I bet you two shillings to a toffee apple he couldn't nick a packet of spam out of Safeways.

What is more revolutionary than the conquest of death?

INTERVIEWER: And what about yourself? apart from appearing on programmes like this...

278: This is just a one-off.

INTERVIEWER: Well, apart from appearing on this.. this one-off, what purpose do you have in living?

278: Life is simply an accumulation of all the forces that resist death. My desire is to make myself a larger part of that process. There's a million million stars for every living thing—feast on their auras and have yourself a fling.

INTERVIEWER: Very poetically put.
With such a unique perspective on the past, on the history of mankind, one wonders why you did not intervene in some of its major disasters—World War 1 and 2 for example. What did you do in the war, daddy?

278: The word War comes from the word **wirra** in Anglo-Saxon, which simply means confusion. How could I have been involved. I believe in order—true order, which is a **dance.** How could I have been involved?

It's hard to teach anyone by example, let alone lemmings. You know what Brecht told me? that all the Jews in Amsterdam were rounded up by letter.. by **letter!** Imagine.

I wrote a little poem on the 27th anniversary of the outbreak of World War 2, which amused me a little. Would you like to hear it?

INTERVIEWER: Certainly.

278: After the success of the 14-18 European Folk Festival, the sponsors spent over twenty years preparing for a global version.

When they held the 39-45 Folk Fest,
a lot of people came,
and a lot of people went.

There was Adolf Church and the Boer Constrictors,
Hyacinth Hitler and the Hog Dodgers,
and many other supporting and suppurating bands—
notably the Bismarck Boasters
and the Soul Spivs.

The music was mainly percussive and full of animosity.
The words in most of the songs, where comprehensible,
seemed to refer to some rift

in the prevailing Judaeo-Christian sub-culture.

The P.A. was poor and in Japan it completely broke
down
and caused brain damage in many heads as yet unspawned.
Many people were forced to grok on the music in over-
crowded compounds
long after they wanted to split.

The Lead Singers were fairly popular
and some of their groupies saw to it that
Hollywood immortalised them in celluloid coffins.
Two or three of them completely burnt themselves out
and died on stage.

The back-up singers and groups got wasted
and flaked out underneath piles of cement crosses
near the main venues,
presumably waiting until the music picked up again.

Many members of the audience had their blood
spiked with lead,
and a host of alien substances by over-zealous
dealers.

There have been many attempts to get the show on
the road again
but even the heaviest backers have now backed out,
feeling that if they held it today,
many people might leave half way,
and the Third World War has been postponed indefinitely
through lack of support.

INTERVIEWER: Is this interview at an end?

278: It's just beginning.

INTERVIEWER: Do you have a last word?

278: I'll leave it with J.B.S.Haldane: *"The universe is not only queerer than we think, it's queerer than we* **can** *think.."* So, don't stop to think. Keep streaming.

There are people alive now who are never going to die.

Put **that** on the news.

(Exit. Fade to Black-Out)